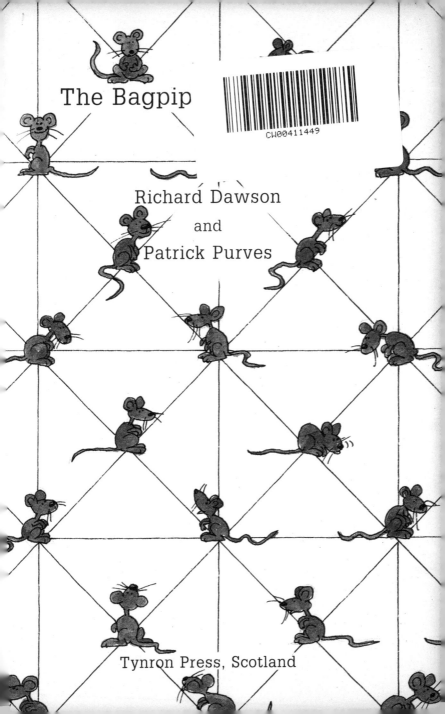

The Bagpip

Richard Dawson

and

Patrick Purves

Tynron Press, Scotland

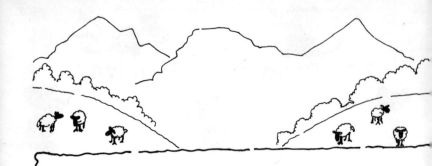

North of the Border in Gorvish Glen,

Bagpiper to the Highland men,

Player to the not-so-squeamish,

Lived the hairy Hamish Beamish

With Tom his son and Lynn his spouse,

In "Hamlyn", as they called their house.

And every year at the Gorvish Games,

He played for Laird and Lady James.

But always in the smoothest ointment

Lurks the fly of disappointment:

The apple of his father's eye,

Tom couldn't play the pipes for pie!

He practised daily in the yard,

But always found the going hard

And though he was given all the kit

He couldn't take to it one little bit.

WEE WEE.....WEEEEE...WEEE...WE...WEE

Now Old MacDonald, a nearby farmer,

Had a piglet, quite a charmer.

The little weaner, known as Pete,

Was always off down Gorvish Street.

One fateful day, by rotten luck,

Pete robbed a dustbin and got stuck.

And Tom, gladly putting down his bag,

Upon his hindlegs went to drag.

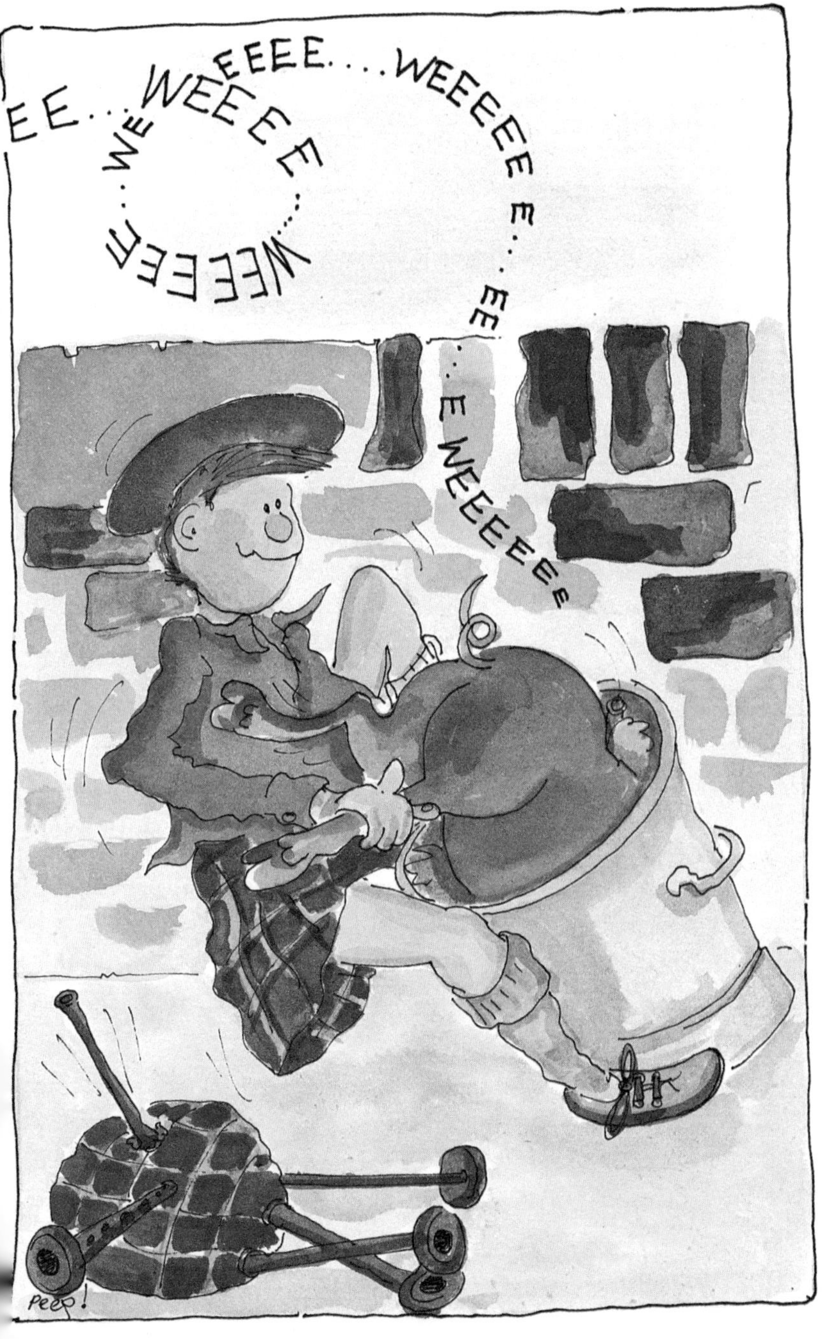
EE...WE...WEEEEE
WEEEEE
EEEE....WEEEEEE E...EE...E WEEEEEEEE
Peep!

The pig came free, with much a-squealing,

Which Hairy Hamish found so appealing;

But Miss McLeod misunderstood,

Thought Tom was up to nothing good,

And cried, "Stop, thief, och, what disaster!"

Poor Tom then started running faster

Followed swiftly by a crowd

Of Gorvish folk, and Miss McLeod.

When all the panic settled down,

And peace returned to Gorvish town,

And Hamish realised the jig

Had been the squealing of a pig,

To Tom these words he sternly spoke:

"Your bagpipe playing is no joke!

There'll be no weekly cash from Daddy,

Until you're playing better, laddie!"

So every night the little fella

Went down to practise in the cellar

And worked away at jigs and reels,

Until one day some different squeals

Made Tom look round, and on the floor

Were rats and mice, fifteen or more.

Some were gazing, others dancing:

They found his playing quite entrancing.

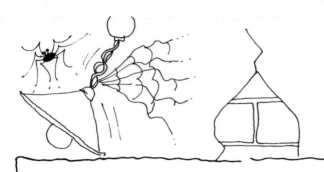

Tom was alarmed, began to run,

Like a tartan bullet from a gun,

And following closely on behind

Came all the mice (Three were quite blind

.... But that's another story!)

When the bagpipes stopped their sound,

Not a rodent could be found.

Tom was sorely shocked and shaken,

But certain he was not mistaken.

From that day forth, while Tom rehearsed,

He almost felt that he was cursed,

For rats and mice in growing numbers

Danced mazurkas, reels and rumbas

All around his piper's brogues,

Behaving just like rogues.

Soon, although the date is vague,

The vermin grew into a plague.

All around the town it seemed,

Rats ran wild and mice just teemed,

Eating all the food supplies,

Gobbling up the Christmas pies.

Rats and mice at every turn,

Up the chimney, down the burn,

In the stable and the manger,

Causing general public danger.

The Laird convened a village meeting:

"This furry lot will take some beating!

Things are going from bad to worse.

What can be done about this curse?"

Tom piped up, "I will remove it!"

All the Elders shouted, "Prove it!"

Tom replied, "No time to waste —

To the Square we must make haste!"

In the Gorvish Central Square,

With all the townsfolk standing there,

Tom blew up the tartan sack,

Hitched his drones onto his back

And started steadily to walk.

The bagpipes didn't squeal or squawk

But rang out with a magical tone,

The chanter quite in tune with the drone.

The people said "That's very well,

And luckily there is no smell!"

Then to their wonder and delight,

Following Tom into the night

Tails a-drag and whiskers solemn,

Marched a mile-long rodent column.

The rats and mice were leaving town.

The Laird cried out, "Make sure they drown!"

Tom led the rats, who led the people,

Past the church with crooked steeple,

Over heather, bog and rock,

Across the hills to Mortish Loch.

Then to the famous Brewer's Leap

The rodent throng did swiftly sweep,

Nor did the host of beasties stop,

When they arrived at Devil's Drop.

At the edge when Tom's march ceased,

The sound of bagpiping increased

And like their European cousins,

Rats and mice in tens and dozens,

Looking neither to left nor right,

Leapt off the cliff into the night,

Never to be seen again,

At least not by the Gorvish men.

(As it turned out, they all could swim,

And passed a cameraman called Jim,

Who took them for an extinct creature,

And filmed them for a double feature.

He sold the pictures to the press,

Claiming he took them on Loch Ness,

And though the monster hunt keeps on,

The rats and mice have long since gone.)

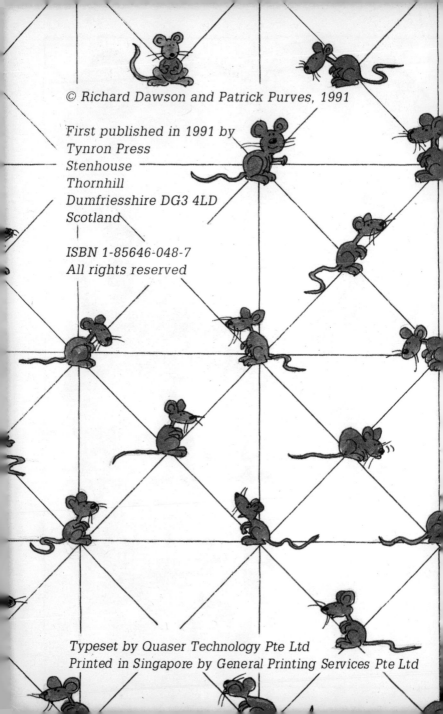

First published in 1991 by
Tynron Press
Stenhouse
Thornhill
Dumfriesshire DG3 4LD
Scotland

ISBN 1-85646-048-7

Typeset by Quaser Technology Pte Ltd
Printed in Singapore by General Printing Services Pte Ltd